LAURENCE ANHOLT was born in London and brought up mostly
in Holland. He studied at Epsom School of Art, Falmouth School
of Art and the Royal Academy. His career has been very varied: as well
as teaching art and exhibiting his paintings, he has worked as a carpenter
and sold encyclopaedias and tropical fish!

Laurence Anholt lives in a rambling farmhouse in Dorset, with his wife,
the writer and illustrator Catherine Anholt, and their three children.
Laurence and Catherine have produced many successful children's picture
books, working both together and separately. Laurence's previous books
for Frances Lincoln include *Can You Guess?* (with Catherine Anholt),
Camille and the Sunflowers and *Degas and the Little Dancer*.

For the children and the trees

First published in Great Britain in 1992 by
Frances Lincoln Limited, 4 Torriano Mews
Torriano Avenue, London NW5 2RZ

First paperback edition 1997

British Library Cataloguing in Publication Data
available on request

ISBN hardback 0-7112-0680-5
ISBN paperback 0-7112-1141-8

Printed in Hong Kong

1 3 5 7 9 8 6 4 2

THE
Forgotten
Forest

Laurence Anholt

FRANCES LINCOLN

A long time ago, but not so far away, there was a country
that was covered by trees.

People used to say that a squirrel could leap from branch to branch, right from one coast to the other.

The great forests were often full of the sounds of
children laughing – and sometimes the chopping of axes

as trees were cleared to make way for houses.
There were so many trees it didn't seem to matter.

And the trees could not complain – even when whole forests were cleared to make way for towns.

Year in, year out. A leaf for every brick.

Until one day there was only a single forest left.

One small forest like an island
in the endless, noisy sea of the city.

And everyone had forgotten it was there.
No one had time to think about trees any more.

Everyone had forgotten – except the children.

Through all the seasons of the year

the children played in the forgotten forest.

Then one day a terrible thing happened. A man hung a notice on the forest fence. It said: BUILDING STARTS TOMORROW.

If the trees could talk they would have cried out then.

The builders opened the gate into the forest . . .
and were amazed by what they found. It was all
so peaceful, so silent.

But listen! There *was* a noise – at first a whispering in the leaves, then a sighing, then a crying. Louder and louder until it sounded as though the whole forest was weeping.

And there in the very centre of the forest were all the children. It was the children crying for the trees.

"Come on!" shouted a man. "We have seen enough."
"Yes!" said the builders. "We must start work straightaway."

But it was not the trees they pulled down –

it was the fence around them.

The children danced with joy – but the work had only just begun. "We will plant new trees!" the builders shouted. "A tree for every child. Trees in every street. Who will help? Will *you* help?"

And in the forgotten forest there was a whispering, then a chuckling. Louder and louder until it sounded as though the whole forest was laughing.
Or was it just the children playing in the trees?

OTHER PICTURE BOOKS IN PAPERBACK FROM FRANCES LINCOLN

RED FOX
Hannah Giffard

A hungry red fox sets out at dusk to find food, but there are no chickens
or fieldmice to eat, only an angry guard dog and a rushing train. So Red Fox
goes to town, where he discovers delicious food for himself and his family.

'The whole effect is original, fresh and sure, with a sweeping fluency.' - Naomi Lewis, *The Observer*

Suitable for National Curriculum English - Reading, Key Stage 1
Scottish Guidelines English Language - Reading, Levels A and B;
Environmental Studies, Levels A and B

ISBN 0-7112-0747-X   £4.99

MOONBEAM'S BIG SPLASH
Jill Dow

One Spring night on Windy Edge Farm, the first calf of the season is born in the
moonlight. Angus names her Moonbeam. What happens when Moonbeam decides
to go exploring, and Angus comes to her rescue, makes perfect bedtime reading
for young Windy Edge fans and newcomers to this popular series.

Suitable for National Curriculum English - Reading, Key Stage 1
Scottish Guidelines English Language - Reading, Level B

ISBN 0-7112-1028-4   £4.99

INDIGO AND THE WHALE
Joyce Dunbar
Illustrated by Geoffrey Patterson

A boy who longs to be a musician . . . a rainbow pipe with magical powers -
Joyce Dunbar's spellbinding story of Indigo, who charms a whale and finds himself
on a journey of self-discovery, will enchant all who read it.

Suitable for National Curriculum English - Reading, Key Stages 1 and 2
Scottish Guidelines English Language - Reading, Level B

ISBN 0-7112-1080-2   £4.99

Frances Lincoln titles are available from all good bookshops.

Prices are correct at time of publication, but may be subject to change.